THE TUB GRANDFATHER

BY PAM CONRAD

ILLUSTRATIONS BY RICHARD EGIELSKI

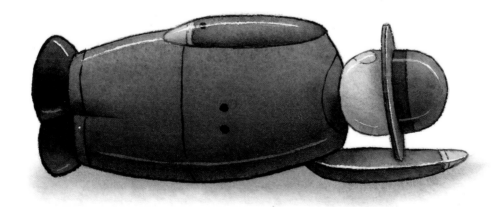

A LAURA GERINGER BOOK
AN IMPRINT OF HARPERCOLLINS PUBLISHERS

The Tub Grandfather
Text copyright © 1993 by Pam Conrad
Illustrations copyright © 1993 by Richard Egielski
Printed in the U.S.A. All rights reserved.

Library of Congress Cataloging-in-Publication Data
Conrad, Pam.
    The Tub grandfather / by Pam Conrad ; illustrations by Richard
Egielski.
        p.   cm.
    Sequel to: The Tub people.
    "A Laura Geringer book."
    Summary: When the Tub Child discovers his missing
grandfather asleep under the radiator, the whole Tub family
rallies to wake him up.
        ISBN 0-06-022895-4. — ISBN 0-06-022896-2 (lib. bdg.)
    [1. Toys—Fiction.   2. Grandfathers—Fiction.]   I. Egielski,
Richard, ill.   II. Title.
PZ7.C76476Tt   1993   92-31770
[E]—dc20   CIP
                                                                AC

Typography by Christine Kettner
1 2 3 4 5 6 7 8 9 10
First Edition

For my daughter Johanna,
with love
—P.C.

For Pam
—R.E.

ONE day the Tub Child led the Tub People in a parade around the rug. There was the mother, the father, the grandmother, the policeman, the doctor and the dog. The Tub Mother made music like a marching flute, and the Tub Father made noise like a marching drum. They all stomped their feet along the edge of the round rug.

The rug was close to the radiator, and under the radiator, near the wall, in the darkness, there lay a little wooden man. He was on his side and covered with dust. He didn't move or make a sound. It was warm under the radiator, warm and dark, and no one had looked there for a long time.

The Tub People did not see him at all.

Soon the Grandmother walked to the center of the rug. "This is a sunny field from long ago," she told them all. "I must plant seeds like I did back then." And she walked along the braided rows, dropping seeds as she went. Her back was to the radiator and she didn't see anyone underneath.

Then the policeman said, "Now it's time to play ball," and when they lined up three by three, the policeman kicked the ball to them. But they missed, and it rolled and rolled, over the rug and across the wooden floor.

It rolled beneath the radiator.

"I'll get it!" called the Tub Child.

He ran across the rug, across the wooden floor and under the radiator.

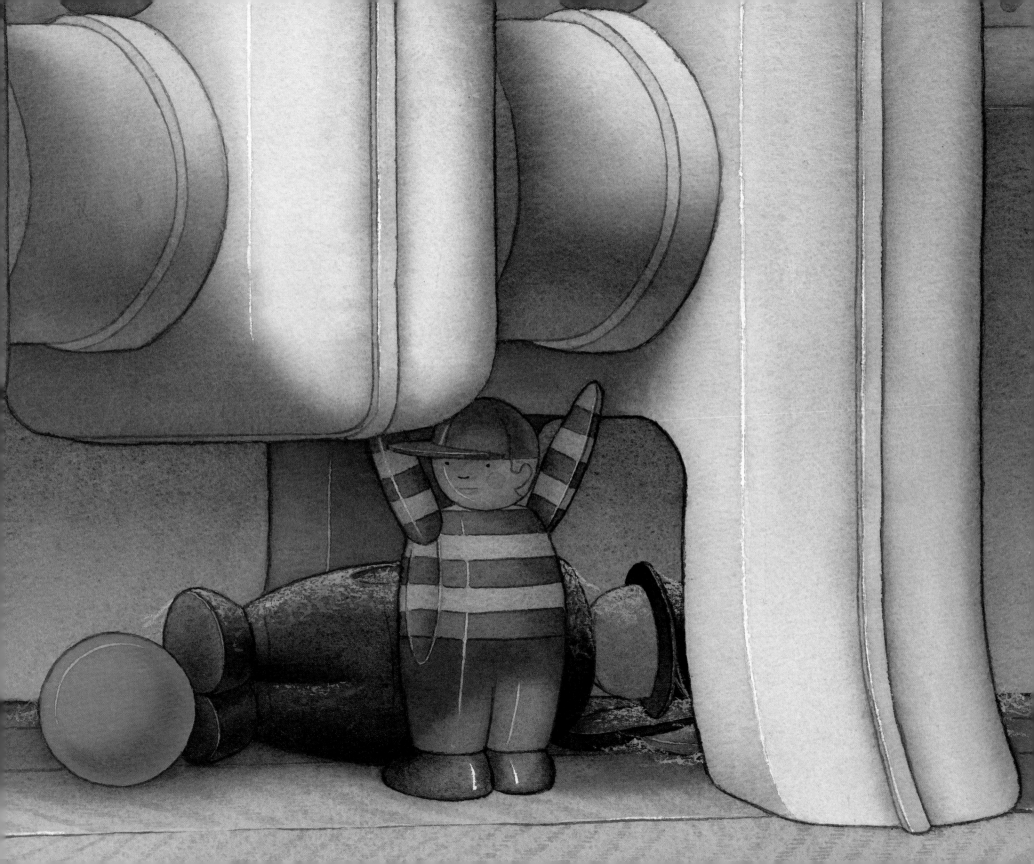

Soon they heard him calling. "Momma."

"Bring out the ball, honey," she said.

"But Momma."

"Hurry," said his father, "before the policeman and the doctor get a home run."

But the Tub Child didn't move. He stood beneath the radiator and stared out at them. "Someone's here," he whispered. "Someone's sleeping in the dust."

"Who?" asked the father.

"Who is it?" the mother asked, coming closer.

The Tub Dog went right up to the little wooden man and sniffed and jumped and barked.

Very carefully the Tub Mother and Tub Father began to roll the little wooden man out from under the radiator.

"Shall I arrest him?" asked the policeman.

"Shall I get a bandage?" asked the doctor.

The Tub Grandmother shushed the dog and leaned over the dusty wooden man who lay on his side.

"Walter?" she whispered. "Walter, dear, is that you?"

But the little wooden man did not answer. Together they rolled him out into the center of the rug where they could see him better. They dusted him off and stood him up. One eye was worn away and the other eye was closed.

The Tub People made a soft circle around him.

"Who's Walter?" asked the Tub Child.

"Your grandfather," the Tub Mother answered, and he stayed very close to her.

"He'll have to open his eye," said the Tub Father. "Let's see if he'll play ball with us."

So they stood the Tub Grandfather at the edge of the rug and rolled the ball to him. It rolled and rolled across the rug and stopped at his feet.

But he did not move. He did not open his eye.

"Oh, dear," sighed the Tub Grandmother.

"A parade!" said the Tub Child, and he began to march along the edge of the rug. "A loud parade!" he said, and one by one the others joined him. They made a very loud parade, but nothing worked. The Tub Grandfather stood woodenly at the edge of the rug and did not open his eye.

Later that night the Tub People lined up along the windowsill. Now there were eight of them—the father, the mother, the grandmother, the doctor, the policeman, the child, the dog and the grandfather. They stood quietly. None of them looked at the Tub Grandfather but they knew his eye was closed.

"There's one more thing we can try," said the policeman in the darkness.

"An ambulance?" asked the doctor.

"Chicken soup?" asked the grandmother.

"The tub," answered the policeman. "Tomorrow we'll take him to the tub."

The next morning the eight Tub People stood along the edge of the bathtub. It was empty and dry. The drain was dark.

"Do you remember this, Walter?" the grandmother asked.

He did not answer.

"Let's go down," said the Tub Father, and at that he slid down the inside of the tub. The Tub Mother followed. Then the grandmother, the doctor, the policeman and the dog all slid down. They waved and called, but the Tub Child and his grandfather stood alone on the edge of the tub.

"I'll watch," said the Tub Child.

The Tub Grandfather said nothing at all. Not even on the edge of the tub.

So back to the round rug they went. They stood the grandfather in the middle and thought about him. There was nothing left to do. Walter, the Tub Grandfather, wouldn't talk, he wouldn't play, and he wouldn't open his eye.

Just then the radiator began to whistle, a low quiet whistle like an old tune. Very slowly, and so slightly you could barely notice, the Tub Grandfather began to rock on his wooden feet.

The Tub Grandmother knew what to do. She went up to her wooden man and began to hum. He opened his eye and looked at her. "Can that be honeysuckle that I smell?" he asked her. She nodded and they began to dance. They danced through all the flowers she had planted in her sunny field from long ago.

The Tub People smiled and quietly watched them. And the tune went on and on.

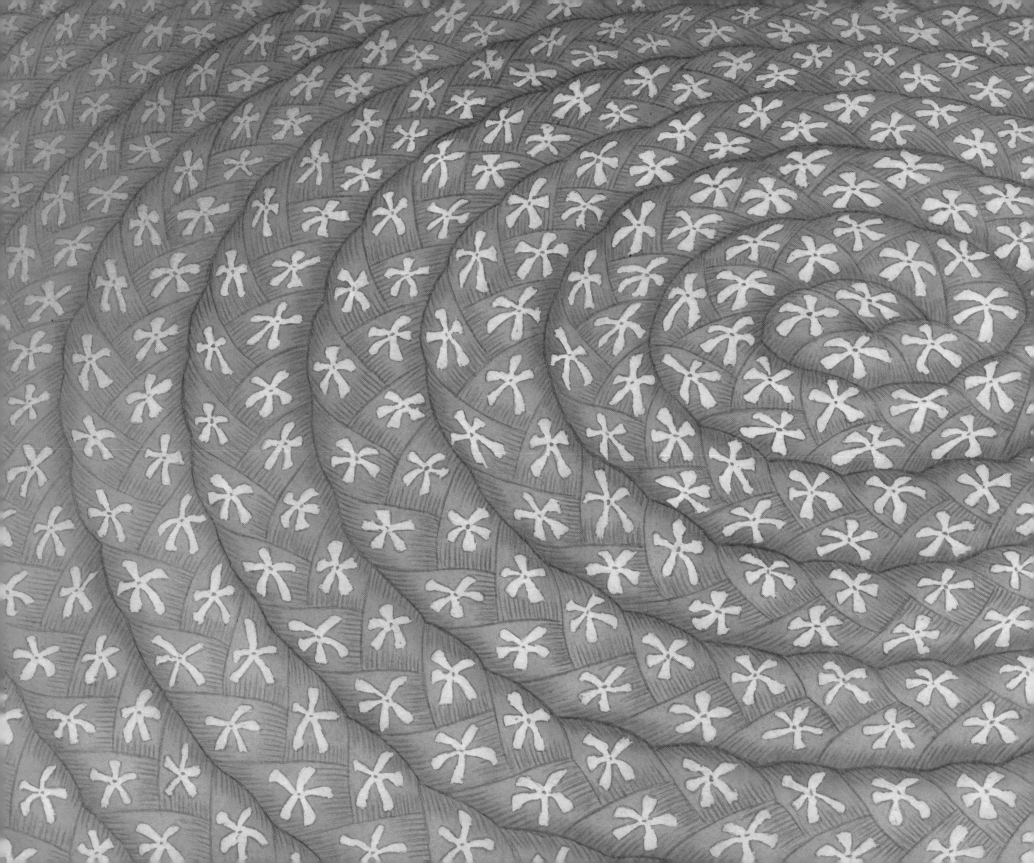

Now at night there are eight Tub People on the windowsill—the father, the mother, the grandmother, the doctor, the policeman, the child, the dog and the grandfather.

And the grandfather still likes to sleep on his side.

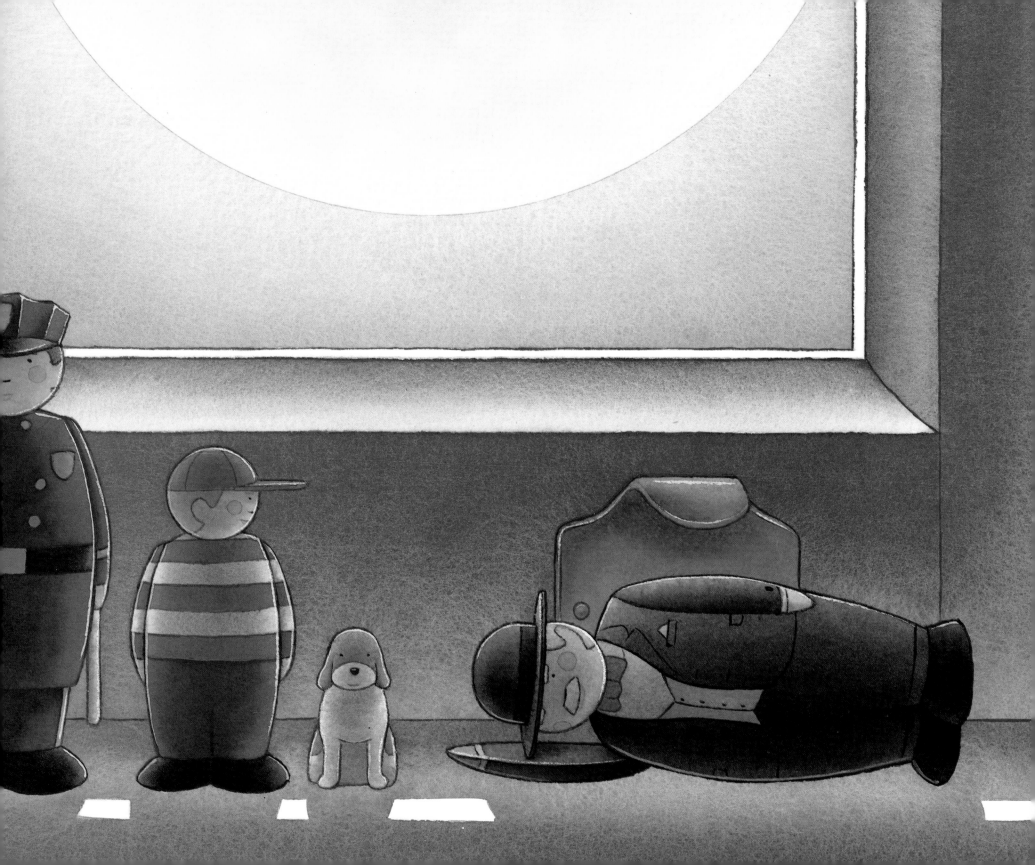